The Story of the Three Little Pigs

With Drawings by

L. Leslie Brooke

The Story of the Three Little Pigs

Copyright © 2013 Lire Books LLC

Illustrated by L. Leslie Brooke

Editor Rachel Drice

Published originally by Frederick Warne & Co. - United Kingdom, United States, c1904.

ISBN-10: 0-9849323-5-6

ISBN-13: 978-0-9849323-5-1

Book Website: www.LireBooks.com
Email: contact@LireBooks.com

Give feedback on the book at:
feedback@LireBooks.com

Printed in U.S.A

Extracts from
"Homage to Leslie Brooke"
an appreciation by M.S. Crouch

"Leslie Brooke was born in 1862 and died in 1940 having ensured for himself a place among the immortals.

There is only a small handful of children's authors and artists whom all children recognize as their friend. Leslie Brooke belongs to this company. The stamp of his personality, lovable, honest and sincere, allied to technical skill of the highest, has resulted in a series of the most delightful books, in which fun and beauty walk hand in hand."

—The Junior Bookshelf

The Story of the Three Little Pigs

Illustrated by L. Leslie Brooke

Lire Books: New York

The Story of
The Three Little Pigs

ONCE upon a time there was an old sow with three little Pigs, and as she had not enough to keep them, she sent them out to seek their fortune.

L·L·B·

The first that went off met a Man with a bundle of straw, and said to him, "Please, Man, give that straw to build me a house"; which the Man did, and the little Pig built a house with it. Presently came along a Wolf, and knocked at the door, and said, "Little Pig, Little Pig, let me come in."

To which the Pig answered, "No, no, by the hair of my chinny chin chin."

"Then I'll huff and I'll puff, and I'll blow your house in!" said the Wolf. so he huffed

and he puffed, and he blew the house in, and ate up the little Pig.

The second Pig met a Man with a bundle of Furze, and said, "Please, Man, give me that furze to build a house"; which the Man did, and the Pig built his house.

Then along came the Wolf and said, "Little Pig, little Pig, let me come in."

"No, no, by the hair of my chinny chin chin."

"Then I'll huff and I'll puff, and I'll blow your house in!" said the Wolf. so he huffed and he puffed, and he blew the house in, and ate up the second little Pig.

The third little Pig met a Man with a load of bricks, and said, "Please, Man, give me those bricks to build a house with"; so the Man gave him the bricks, and he built his house with them. So the Wolf came, as he did to the other Pigs, and said, "Little Pig, Little Pig, let me come in."

"No, no, by the hair of my chinny chin chin."

"Then I'll huff and I'll puff, and I'll blow your house in."

Well he huffed and he puffed, and he huffed and he puffed, and he puffed and he huffed; but he could not get the house down. When he found that he could not, with all his huffing and puffing, blow the house down, he said, "Little Pig, I know where there is a nice field of turnips."

"Where?" said the little Pig.

"Oh, in Mr. Smith's home-field; and if you will be ready to-morrow morning, I will call for you, and we will go together and get some dinner."

"Very well," said the little Pig, "I will be ready. What time do you mean to go?"

"Oh, at six o'clock."

Well, the little Pig got up at five, and got the turnips as was home again before six. When the Wolf came he said, "little Pig, rare you ready?"

"Ready!" said the little Pig, "I have been and come back again, and got a nice pot-full for dinner."

The Wolf felt very angry at this, but thought that he would be *up to* the little Pig somehow or other; so he said, "Little Pig, I know where there is a nice apple-tree."

"Where?" said the Pig.

"Down at Merry-garden," replied the Wolf; "and if you will not deceive me I will come for you, at five o'clock to-morrow, and we will go together and get some apples."

Well, the little Pig woke at four the next morning, and bustled up, and went off for the apples, hoping to get back before the Wolf came, but he had farther to go,

and had climb the tree, so that just as he was coming down from it, he saw the wolf coming, which, as you may supposes, frightened him very much. When the Wolf came up he said, "Little Pig, what! are you here before me? Are they nice apples?"

"Yes, very," said the little Pig; "I will throw you down one." And he threw it so far that, while the Wolf was gone to pick it up, the little Pig jumped down and ran home.

The next day the Wolf came again, and said to the little Pig, "Little Pig, there is a Fair in the Town this afternoon: will you go?"

"Oh, yes," said the Pig, "I will go; what time shall you be ready?"

"At three," said the Wolf.

So the little Pig went off before the time, as usual, and got to the Fair, and bought a butter churn, and was on his way home with it when he saw the Wolf coming. Then he could not tell what to do. So he got into the churn to hide, and in doing so turned it

L.L.B.

young, and it began to roll, and rolled down hill with the Pig inside it, which frightened the Wolf so much that he ran home without going to the Fair.

He went to the little Pig's house, and told him how frightened he had been by a great round thing which came down the hill past him.

Then the little Pig said, "Hah! I frightened you, did I? I had been to the Fair and bought a butter churn, and when I saw you I got into it, and rolled down the hill."

Then the Wolf was very angry indeed, and declared he *would* eat up the little Pig, and that he would get down the chimney after him.

When the little Pig saw what he was about, he hung on the pot full of water, and made up a blazing fire, and, just as the Wolf was coming down, took off the cover of the pot, and in fell the Wolf. And the little Pig put on the cover again in an instant, boiled him up, and ate him for supper, and lived happy ever after.

The End

More Classic Storybooks
Published by Lirebooks.com

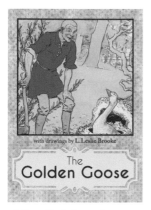

The Golden Goose
By L. Leslie Brooke

Little Red Riding
Hood - Retold

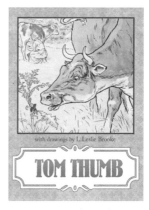

Tom Thumb
By L. Leslie Brooke

The Tailor & the Crow
By L. Leslie Brooke

Tales of Enchant-
ment from Spain
By Elsie Spicer Eells

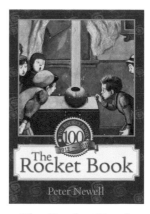

The Rocket Book
by Peter Newell

CPSIA information can be obtained
at www.ICGtesting.com
Printed in the USA
LVHW071737131118
596978LV00015B/145/P